THE TURBULENT

TWIN

TRUTH REVEALED

PART TWO

JUDITH G H MCCULLUM

Published by Hemingway Publishers

Cover design by Hemingway Publishers

ISBN: Printed in the United States

Contents

CHAPTER ONE

Janet couldn't believe what she was hearing; she just stood there in shock. *How could this be happening*, she thought. She couldn't speak. The young woman was staring at her, waiting for a response.

Janet swallowed, and with her voice shaking, she said, "How, how did you find me?"

"Well, actually, it wasn't difficult, now that all birth records are available. I must say, though, I didn't expect to find you so soon."

Janet was clearly struggling to respond.

Jane, who was standing in the background, stepped in. "Paula, you said your name was Paula, right? Please come in, we were just relaxing in the living room. Please take a seat. Can I get you a cup of tea?"

Janet stood watching, overwhelmed and thinking to herself. *OH MY GOD, I can't believe this is happening*, and then the questions started in her mind, and most of all, she asked herself, "Where is this all going?" She thought of Bobby, who now has a daughter, and Aunt Ruth, and *my bio mom is a grandmother*. She started to laugh, and she couldn't stop.

They all turned and looked at her with annoyance, but

when the laughter became hysterical, they became concerned. Ruth went over to Janet, saying, "Janet, stop, please stop. Are you alright? Jane, get her a glass of water."

Paula spoke up, saying, "I'm so sorry, this is all my fault, I'll leave."

Janet then regained her composure. "No, I'm sorry, please, please don't go. I'm okay, it was just a shock, that's all. Please stay, we would love to talk to you."

Paula couldn't help thinking maybe this was a mistake. *Something's not right. I can feel a strange vibe.*

Jane spoke up and asked, "Paula, Janet, would you two like some privacy? Aunt Ruth and I will be in the kitchen."

After Jane and Ruth left, Janet turned to Paula. "I'm so sorry for that outburst earlier. I don't handle surprises very well, and also my mum just passed away this week, so my head isn't in a good place right now."

"I'm so sorry, my timing couldn't be worse. I do understand, I can relate, I was quite shocked when I learned I was adopted."

Janet replied, "So your adoptive parents recently told you?"

"No, no, they didn't, actually, I found the adoption papers in a safe. You see, my parents, or I guess I should say, my adoptive parents were killed in a car accident. Being the only child, they left everything to me, as was stated in the will.

Also, the will contained the adoption papers."

Janet couldn't help feeling sympathetic. "Oh, Paula, I'm sorry you had to go through all that."

"Thank you, I'm fine, it's been three years since the accident. I think it's best if I leave now; you have enough to deal with. I hope we can meet again."

"Yes, absolutely, I would love to see you again. I won't be here in Chelmsford for much longer; I live in New York City. So once everything calms down, we should plan a get-together with family."

"Oh, that sounds lovely. Here's my phone number. Please say goodbye to Jane and Ruth for me."

"Yes, yes, of course." Reaching the door, they said their goodbyes. Janet stood in the doorway watching as Paula climbed into her car and drove away. Overwhelmed with emotion, she couldn't stop the tears that erupted into heart-wrenching sobs. She then felt Ruth's comforting arms wrap around her, holding her close.

Ruth realized this was the first time she actually held her daughter. "Janet, sweetheart, it's going to be okay, it'll all work out."

"It's just too much all at once. I'm having a hard time with mum dying, and learning that she wasn't my mother. I feel so bad for all that I put her through. Then there's the fact that Jane and I are half-sisters… not twins. Aunt Ruth, it's hard… and I don't know what to call you now." She broke down crying again.

"Janet, it doesn't matter what you call me. Just know that I'm always here for you."

Jane also tried comforting Janet. "I'm here too, Janet, and nothing has changed. I'll always be your sister, and know that I love you."

Ruth then suggested that Janet go upstairs and lie down.

After Janet went upstairs, Jane turned to Ruth. "Oh, Aunt Ruth, I'll have to tell Bobby, and we have to tell Dad when he gets home… hopefully before Janet comes back downstairs."

"Yes, dear, we'll tell him together."

At that moment, they heard the back door open and close. Liam entered the living room. "Everyone okay, you're awfully quiet?"

Jane and Ruth exchanged glances, and then Jane spoke up. "Well, Dad, I hope you had a relaxing time on the golf course because Aunt Ruth and I have news for you."

"News, good news I hope… I don't think I could handle any more bad news."

"No, Dad, it's not bad news, but it is surprising."

"What is it, tell me?"

"Well, first of all, we had a visitor while you were out. A young lady showed up at the front door asking for Janet…

claiming to be her daughter."

"What did you just say?"

"I know it's a lot to take in… though it seems that you are a grandfather."

"How can this be? How did she find her?"

"Well, apparently, birth records are now available to children who were given up for adoption. The only address they had was this one, and with Janet being home, it was easy for her to find her."

"So where is she? Where's Janet? Did they go somewhere?"

"No, Dad, Janet is upstairs lying down; it was quite a shock for her, to say the least."

"What about the girl? Did she just leave? What took place? Oh, I wish I had been here. I would love to meet her."

"I'm sure that will happen. Janet needs time to process all of this information; it's been a lot for her to take in, considering everything else that's going on."

"Yes, yes of course, I get it. So, will she be in touch with her? Oh, and what is her name?"

"She said her name was Paula Peterson, and before she left, she gave Janet her phone number where she could be reached."

"That's it? You just let her walk away? You didn't

welcome her in?"

"Yes, Dad, we did, and Aunt Ruth and I left her and Janet alone in the living room. We thought it was best for them to talk privately. Then the next thing we hear is Janet sobbing her heart out, and Paula is gone. We need to give Janet some space with this."

"Yes, you're right… So, you have to tell Bobby he has a daughter."

"I know, Dad, I plan on telling him tonight as soon as he gets home from work."

CHAPTER TWO

Upon arriving home and unlocking her front door, Jane went directly to her favourite spot in the house… her sunroom. After sitting down in her wicker chair, she felt the stress leaving her body. There was so much to think about. She had mixed feelings about telling Bobby the big news. Especially since she and Bobby never had any children. They both decided after they were married that it wouldn't be fair to any child to have parents who were so committed to their careers. After closing her eyes, she soon fell asleep.

"Jane, wake up, honey. Are you okay?"

"Oh, Bobby, you're home, I must have fallen asleep, what a day it's been."

"I can only imagine it must have been so hard going through your mother's belongings."

"That was only the half of it."

"Why, what's going on now? Wait, let me guess, it has something to do with Janet, am I right?"

"I'm afraid so… but it isn't just Janet… it concerns all of us."

"What are you talking about, Jane? What would concern us? Does it have something to do with your mum's passing? Was there something in the will?"

"No, Bobby, nothing like that. It's about the baby Janet gave up for adoption… your baby!"

"What, why is this coming up now?"

"Well, she isn't a baby anymore. She's a young lady of twenty-three. We were just finishing up with mum's things when the doorbell rang, and there she was, asking for Janet and claiming to be her daughter. Which means… your daughter."

"Oh, MY, God, tell me, what happened next, how did Janet react?"

"It wasn't good. Janet was in a state of shock. We managed to calm her down, and they did have a talk, and before she left, she gave Janet a phone number where she could be reached. After she left, Janet went upstairs to lie down. Then Dad came home, and we broke the news to him. Dad wants to meet her, but Aunt Ruth and I think it's best to wait and see what Janet wants."

"Wow, this is crazy. I never expected anything like this."

"I don't think any of us did. I guess we'll just have to wait and see what Janet wants to do."

"I don't think so. This is my daughter too. I need to find out more than this."

"You will, Bobby, but you need to be patient."

CHAPTER THREE

Turning into the hotel parking lot, Paula thought to herself, *Well, that certainly wasn't the reunion I was hoping for. I guess one never knows what to expect in a situation like this.* As she unlocked the door to her hotel room, she was thankful that her fiancé had insisted on coming with her, even though she wanted to do this on her own.

"Paula, you're back. Sooo, how did you make out? Did you have any luck with the address you found?"

"Yes, I did, but it was a little strange, you could say."

"Strange how? Did you find her?"

"Oh yes, I found her. The address was her childhood home, and she was there because her mother had just passed away. She was there to be with her family."

"Wow, that's great. I mean that she was there when you went searching. That's too bad about her mother. Oh, yes, she would have been your grandmother. So, tell me, what was her reaction when you told her who you are?"

"Well, to say the least, she was shocked. A lady answered the door, and when I told her I was looking for Janet Johnson, she invited me in. When Janet came to the door, she asked why I wanted to see her. I then told her who I was and that I had adoption papers stating that she was my birth-mother. She never said anything, and then she started to laugh… hysterically. Thank God her sister was there, the one who answered the door… Oh, and another lady, whom they called Aunt Ruth. So, they calmed her down and explained that she had been through a lot the past month. I'm not sure what it was about aside from her mother dying. She did calm down and apologize after they invited me inside. We spoke briefly, and she asked where she could reach me. I gave her the phone number of the hotel room. I suppose it was a lot to take in, especially after just losing her mom. Oh, Daniel, I do hope she calls."

CHAPTER FOUR

As Janet entered the bedroom she grew up in, she had an overwhelming feeling of nostalgia. Lying down on the bed, she closed her eyes, but couldn't rest. Thoughts of her mother triggered tears and regret. "Oh, mum, I'm so sorry for all that I put you through. I was such a brat, so mean to Jane, sneaking out of the house when you thought I was in bed asleep. Going to parties, doing drugs and drinking. How disappointed you must have been when I got pregnant at sixteen, after I seduced Jane's boyfriend at a party, knowing Jane was at home. Oh, Mum, how could you ever forgive me for all of that? I don't blame you for sending me away to the home for unwed mothers. What I must have put you through when I came home… overdosing on drugs and then running away from the hospital. When the police showed up with a warning the day you were to take me home, I just felt I needed to get as far away as possible. Running away to New York City to Aunt Ruth's seemed like the only way out. Oh, Mum, how hurt you must have been when you found out that Dad and Aunt Ruth had a one-night fling and they kept it hidden all those years, all the time, knowing I was Ruth's daughter… not yours. Mum, I'm so sorry, and I miss you so, so much. Mum, I need you to help me do the right thing concerning Paula. I'm afraid of what this might do to Jane and Bobby; then again, it might all work out for the best. I do hope so."

Janet woke up to darkness and a damp pillow. She then heard a soft tap on the bedroom door and Aunt Ruth's voice, "Janet, are you awake? Jane and Bobby are downstairs, and they want to talk."

"I'll be right down, just give me a minute."

"Okay, dear, I'll tell them."

When Janet entered the living room, there was Bobby, Jane, her dad and Aunt Ruth. They were all talking in hushed tones; Janet cleared her throat, "Ahem, ahem."

Ruth looked up. "Come in and sit down, Janet. I hope you're feeling better. We were just talking about Paula, and if it's okay with you, we have a suggestion."

"Janet looked directly at Bobby and asked, "Oh, and what would that be, Bobby? I assume Jane has filled you in on what took place earlier today."

"Yes, Janet, she did. She told me everything about Paula showing up, and looking for her birth-mother."

Jane then spoke up, "Well, Janet, we all think it would be a nice idea if you reached out to Paula and invited her here so she could meet Bobby and Dad."

"Yes, I can do that. I'll call her tonight, and hopefully she can come tomorrow. I'm not sure how long she is staying in New England, and Ruth and I also need to get back to New York. Now, if you don't mind, I'll say goodnight, and as soon as I speak to Paula, I'll let you know."

Janet had so much going on in her head, she didn't know where to start. She thought of her friend Kathy, and oh, how she wished she could sit and talk to her. Kathy always knew what to say to make her feel better. She then thought of how nice it would be to get back to New York. Oh, how she missed the hustle and bustle of New York City. Living there was magical, and she felt so free; she could just be herself, with no judgment from anyone.

Noticing the phone was still in her old bedroom, she called the number Paula gave her. She couldn't help but feel nervous when the phone started ringing.

"Hello."

Janet, recognizing Paula's voice, said, "Paula, it's Janet here. I'm so glad I caught you. My family and I were wondering if you could come over tomorrow? My dad is so looking forward to meeting you, and so are my sister Jane and Aunt Ruth. They would love to have another chance to get to know you. Paula, I must apologize again for my behaviour when you were here. I'm feeling better now, and I would love for you to come and meet everyone."

"Oh my… yes… yes, of course, I would be delighted to meet with everyone. My fiancé is here, and he will be with me if that's okay? Oh, what time would you like us there?"

"Let's say around two o'clock, and yes, by all means, bring your fiancé, we would like that."

"Okay, two o'clock, that's perfect. We'll see you then."

"Paula, before you hang up, there is someone else who will be here: Jane's husband, Bobby. Paula, you should know that Bobby… is your biological father, and he is very anxious to meet you. I know this is a lot to take in, and I'm sorry you're learning this over the phone. I just wanted to prepare you for tomorrow."

"Oh my, I get it, and yes, I would be delighted to meet him. I have to say I never expected this, this is so exciting! Oh, Janet, I can't wait! See you tomorrow at two."

"Yes, I'm looking forward to seeing you both as well. Bye for now."

After hanging up the phone, Janet suddenly felt totally exhausted, but in a good way. Hurrying down the stairs, she called out to Aunt Ruth and her dad. "I have news."

"We're in the living room, Janet."

"Oh, there you are. It's all set, Paula and her fiancé are coming tomorrow at two o'clock."

Liam and Ruth both spoke at once. "Oh, Janet, that's wonderful!" Liam jumped up, giving Janet a big hug. "I can't wait to meet my granddaughter, and she is bringing her fiancé. Wow, this family is growing."

CHAPTER FIVE

As Paula was hanging up the phone, she turned, and Daniel, who was right behind her, said, "Well, you look happy. What did she say? Are we going to meet them tomorrow?"

"Oh, Daniel, I'm so excited, you won't believe what she told me."

"Tell me… don't keep me in suspense."

"Well, not only will I get to meet my grandfather, but my biological father will also be there, and that's not all…"

"What, what else did she tell you?"

"My biological father is married to her sister, who is also my aunt. This just gets better and better. Oh, Daniel, I can't wait!"

CHAPTER SIX

The next morning, Janet was up before the sun, even though she barely slept—so many thoughts spinning around in her head. She had a strange feeling in her gut telling her something wasn't right, but then again, maybe she was just imagining it. On her way downstairs, she could hear her dad and Aunt Ruth talking in the kitchen. She hesitated on the stairs, trying to make out what they were saying.

"Ruth, can you believe this? I'm just so excited to meet this girl, my granddaughter… our granddaughter. I'm afraid there's going to be a lot of explaining to do."

"Liam, what do you mean 'explaining'?"

"Well, she's going to want to know the truth of her biological family."

"Oh, Liam, wait a minute. This isn't up to us. Janet has enough on her plate with Jane and Bobby. Don't even think about how you and I are involved in this."

"Yes, you're right. We should just stay in the background for now."

Janet breathed a sigh of relief. Walking into the kitchen, she couldn't keep quiet. "Good morning, you two. I couldn't help overhearing all that. Dad, you need to listen to Aunt Ruth. I can't get into all that just yet, like Aunt Ruth said, I have enough to explain to Paula as it is."

"Yes, Janet, I agree, I'm just so excited about her finding us, that's all."

"I understand, Dad, I do, and we will get there when the time is right, I promise."

CHAPTER SEVEN

They all gathered in the living room, waiting for the doorbell to ring. Janet felt anxious but excited at the same time. Looking around, she could see the others were also looking forward to the meeting, especially her dad, who was sitting in the chair by the window watching for them. "Oh, I think they're here, there's a car turning in the driveway."

"Okay, Dad, stay seated please, I'll get the door."

Just then, the doorbell rang. Janet jumped up to answer the door, and standing on the front step were her daughter and her fiancé. Janet couldn't help feeling overwhelmed. "Oh, Paula, it's so lovely to see you again."

"Yes, you too, Janet, and I'd like you to meet my fiancé, Daniel Lombardo."

"So nice to meet you, Daniel. Please come in, the others are waiting in the living room."

Liam, with arms wide open, reached out to Paula. "I'm Liam, your grandfather, and I have to say, what a joyous occasion this is."

"Yes, for me too, Grandpa. Is it okay if I call you 'Grandpa'?"

"Yes, absolutely, I would love that. Oh, so I understand you already met Ruth and Jane, and this is Jane's husband

Bobby."

Paula brushes tears aside, saying, "Oh, it's so wonderful to meet you all, and to know that we're family."

Janet, being curious, asked Paula, "Do you have relatives from your previous family, other than your parents?"

"No, it was just me and my parents. Now knowing I have all of you as family, I can't begin to tell you how much this means to me."

Liam spoke up, "I hope this means we'll see you often? Where do you live, Paula? I hope it's not too far away?"

"We live in Boston, so no, it's not too far."

Meanwhile, Jane and Bobby sat quietly, not saying a word. After more small talk about Boston and how the Red Sox were doing in the new season, Bobby couldn't hold back any longer.

"Paula, I don't believe you're aware of our connection."

"Well, actually, Janet did tell me last night, and I can't believe my luck in finding you all at the same time."

Bobby immediately stood up, reaching out for a hug, and Paula didn't hesitate to respond. "Does this mean I can call you 'Dad'?"

"Absolutely, I would be honored."

Ruth then stood up, saying, "This calls for a celebration, let's have a toast… to new beginnings!"

CHAPTER EIGHT

Janet was feeling sooo tired, but in a good way. Oh, the emotion in the room tonight was overwhelming, but thank God, Dad and Ruth didn't bring up their story. Lots of time for that to come out. Lying there in bed, she thought she should call Kathy and let her know she's coming home. *I need to get back to my life in New York; this town has too much baggage. I'll call tomorrow, too tired tonight.*

The next morning, Janet woke again to the hushed voices of her dad and Aunt Ruth. *Oh no, not again.* She decided to call Kathy right away and tell Aunt Ruth it was time to go home, the sooner the better, but only after talking to Kathy, who was delighted to hear she was coming home and couldn't wait to hear Janet's big news.

Entering the kitchen, she just shook her head. They looked like a couple of schemers. After clearing her throat, she quietly asked, "And what are you two up to now?"

Liam, looking a bit guilty, said, "Oh, not much, dear, we were just wondering when we would see Paula and Daniel again."

"Oh, Dad, there's lots of time. I think we need to let things settle for a bit. Also, you should know, Ruth and I think it's time we headed back to the city. Aunt Ruth, I spoke to Kathy this morning to let her know we would be back today."

"Yes, dear, I agree, we need to get back home. I'll go upstairs now and pack."

After pouring herself a cup of coffee, Janet turned to her dad. "Dad, are you going to be okay? You've been through a lot the past few weeks?'

"Oh, Janet, I'll be fine. It's been a lot for all of us, but having Paula turn up right after losing your mother was like a sign, don't you think?"

"You know I never thought of it like that, but maybe you're right."

"I'll miss you, Janet, and please don't take so long to come home again."

"I'll try, Dad, I'll try. You know, you could come to New York."

"Yeah, I just might. I've always wanted to see the Big Apple."

"Okay then, we'll work on that. I should get ready. Ruth will be down in a minute, ready and waiting."

It was a tearful goodbye as the three of them stood on the front porch, giving one last hug. "Take care, Dad and keep in touch."

"You too, Janet and you as well, Ruth."

As they drove away, Janet felt some relief knowing Jane and Bobby were nearby for her father. She was confident they would keep an eye on him.

CHAPTER NINE

For Janet, driving into New York City was like a new beginning; she felt so free, free of guilt, secrets, and all the hurt she caused her family. She could finally put that all behind her.

Arriving at Janet's apartment building, Ruth parked the car, saying, "We're home, Janet."

"Oh, Aunt Ruth, thank you for everything. You know it doesn't feel right for me to call you Aunt Ruth. Would it be okay if I just call you Ruth?"

"Yes, Janet, I would be fine with that, whatever makes you comfortable."

"Okay, Ruth, thank you again, and we will be in touch soon."

Unlocking her apartment door, Janet called out, "Kathy, I'm home!"

Kathy came running to meet her; "Oh, Janet, I'm so glad you're back, and everyone at work will be too. They keep asking me when Janet is coming back."

"Oh, Kathy, it's so good to be back. I have so much to tell you, you won't believe what took place. I'll just unpack and then we can sit and have a chat over a glass of wine."

Kathy was shocked to hear what took place with Janet. "Oh my God, Janet, that's crazy. I'm so sorry about your mum. Oh, you must have been in shock when Paula showed up, especially just days after losing your mum."

"Yes, it was a shock, but I did manage to pull myself together, with Jane and Ruth's help."

"So what happens now? When will you see her again?"

"I'm not sure. She and her fiancé live in Boston, which isn't too far away. She said she would be in touch, so I guess I'll just have to wait and see."

"Oh, Janet, what about your Aunt Ruth? That must be awkward. What are you going to call her?"

"Oh, Kathy, I don't know, but I do know I can't call her Aunt Ruth. I guess I'll just refer to her as Ruth."

"Sooo, does Paula know that Ruth is your biological mother?"

"Oh, no. That will have to wait for another time. I couldn't get into that. I'm still trying to wrap my head around it."

"Yes, I can only imagine. So you mentioned they live in Boston, you know that's where I'm from. What are their last names?"

"Paula's last name is Peterson, and when she introduced Daniel, I think she said his last name was Lombardo."

"Really? Well, that name is known in certain areas of Boston."

"So, Kathy, tell me what's new at work? Why don't you fill me in on all the gossip? I can't wait to hear what's been going on."

CHAPTER TEN

The next morning, as Paula and Daniel made their way to the nearest restaurant for breakfast, Paula couldn't help noticing how quiet Daniel had been since arriving back at the hotel the night before. "Daniel, you're very quiet. Are you okay?"

"I'm fine, Paula, a little worried about you. When do you think you can tell them why you needed to find blood relatives?"

"Well, I don't know, maybe when we meet with them again. I do have three relatives here: my grandfather, my mother, two aunts, and my father. Oh my God, Daniel, maybe I have two more; Daniel's parents, they would be my grandparents. Oh, this just gets better and better… Surely one of them would be a match. I'll call my grandfather and arrange another meeting, and I'll explain what's going on."

"Paula, I don't think you should wait any longer. You know what the doctor said: the sooner the better."

"Yes, Daniel, I know, it's just hard. I don't want them to think that's the only reason I turned up looking for them."

"Oh, Paula, I'm sure they will understand."

"I hope you're right."

When Liam arrived home, he could hear the phone

ringing as he stepped inside the door. Rushing into the living room, he picked up the phone. "Hello."

"Hi Grandpa, it's Paula. I was wondering if we could have another get-together before Daniel and I have to go back to Boston?"

"Oh my, yes, absolutely. Would you like me to ask Jane and Bobby to be there too?"

"Yes, I would if they could make it. There is something important that I need to discuss with all of you."

"Oh, okay. I hope it's nothing too serious. I can give them a call. When would you like to meet?"

"I was thinking tonight if that works. Daniel and I have to get back to Boston before the end of the week, so we don't have a lot of time."

"I understand. I'll give them a call, and as soon as I hear from them, I'll get back to you."

"That sounds great, Grandpa, thank you."

"No thanks necessary, I'll be in touch."

Jane and Bobby were relaxing on their deck with Bobby's parents, who were over the moon to learn that they had a granddaughter. Bobby's mom was so excited. "When can we meet her? Where are they staying, and how long will they be here in New England?"

"Mum, please, we should hear from them soon, so as soon

as we get a call, I'll let you know."

Bobby then heard the phone ringing. "I hear the phone; I'll be right back." Bobby returned with a big smile on his face; "Guess what, we're going to meet with Paula and Daniel tonight at Liam's. What do you think?"

Bobby's parents jumped up and held Bobby in a big hug. Bobby's mum, wiping tears from her eyes, exclaimed, "Oh, Bobby, this is wonderful! I can't wait to meet her."

CHAPTER ELEVEN

Paula was feeling anxious about telling them what the other reason was to find them. Then again, they all seemed genuinely sincere about their feelings for her. She didn't have a choice, and she knew she couldn't put it off any longer. She hoped they would understand.

When she and Daniel drove into the driveway, they could see that the others were already there. As they entered the front porch, the door swung open, and there was Liam, smiling from ear to ear.

"Welcome, Paula and Daniel, so good to see you again. Come on in, the others are waiting for you." Entering the house, everyone was standing, waiting to greet them. Bobby was quick to introduce Paula to his parents, who reached out with hugs. Bobby's mum exclaimed, "Oh, Paula, this is such a wonderful surprise, you have no idea what this means to us!"

Paula, trying not to get too emotional, smiled, saying, "Yes, me too, and I'd like you to meet Daniel, my fiancé."

Bobby's father spoke up, asking, "Daniel… and your last name?"

Daniel then came forward with his hand extended. "Oh yes, Lombardo, Daniel Lombardo. So nice to meet you."

After shaking hands, Liam suggested they go into the

living room and take a seat. After everyone was seated, Liam, being curious, looked at Paula and said, "So, Paula, we have so many questions, I hope you're okay with that?"

"Yes, of course, I totally understand. You can ask me anything you wish."

"Well, I'm just wondering why you didn't start searching for your birth-mother when you found out you were adopted?"

"Yes, well, like I told Janet, my adoptive parents were killed in a car accident two years ago. I wasn't aware that I was adopted until I found the papers while sorting through their belongings. I must say it came as quite a shock. I was grieving the loss of my parents, only to discover they weren't my biological parents. Also, I was still going to university, studying for my nursing degree. I was curious about my background, but I just wasn't ready to go there."

Jane and Bobby exchanged glances before Bobby spoke up, "Paula, that is wonderful that you have a career in nursing. It just so happens that I'm a doctor, and Jane is also a registered nurse. I guess practising medicine runs in the family. Do you work in private practice or at a hospital?"

"I've been at the Massachusetts Hospital since I graduated.

Liam interrupted as he couldn't hold back any longer. "So, Paula, you mentioned there was something you wanted to discuss with us?"

"Yes, there is, and I want to be clear, this isn't the only reason I came searching for you. I very much wanted to find my biological family, and then I learned that I have ESRD or End-Stage Renal Disease. My doctor tells me I need to find a donor as soon as possible. My doctor asked if I had any siblings or family members who might want to donate one of their kidneys. I thought maybe the hospital would find a donor, but my doctor assured me that a family member would be a closer match than a stranger. After discovering that I have blood relatives, I just might have a match. I understand this is a lot to take in, and I completely understand if you think I'm expecting way too much from any of you."

Bobby was the first to speak up, "You can count on me, Paula. I can get tested as soon as you need me to."

Liam then spoke up, "Count me in, too, Paula."

Bobby's parents spoke up at the same time, "Me too, Paula, just say where and when."

Jane also declared, "You can count on me, too, Paula."

Paula, becoming very emotional, trying to hold back the tears, replied, "Oh my, this is absolutely amazing that all of you are so willing to give me this enormous gift."

They all spoke at once, "You're family, Paula, and that's what families do."

"Paula, does Janet know about this?" Jane asked.

"No, she doesn't. I was hoping she would still be here in

New England. I guess she had to get back to work."

Liam then spoke up, "Yes, Paula, Janet had to get back to New York City. She is one of the managers at Macy's Department Store. She had taken a leave of absence when Anne was ill, so she thought it was time she got back to work."

Bobby then suggested he would contact Janet and Ruth. "If that's okay with you, Paula, I can also make the arrangements with the hospital for all of them to have blood samples taken, and the results sent to your doctor in Boston."

"That sounds wonderful, I can't believe this is happening!" Paula exclaimed.

"I'll contact my doctor as soon as I get home. I just hope Janet and Ruth don't feel left out due to them not being here."

Bobby tried to reassure her, saying, "I'm sure they will understand, Paula, and as a doctor, I will explain everything to the best of my ability."

Paula reached out to Bobby, giving him a big hug. "Thank you, Dad, you're the best." Paula and Daniel decided it was time to say their goodbyes. They too needed to get back home, Daniel stating, "Duty calls."

"Daniel, you never mentioned what it is you do for a living?" Bobby asked.

"I'm an attorney, family-owned business."

"Oh, good for you, your family must be so proud."

"I suppose they are, and hopefully, you'll all get to meet them soon."

As Paula and Daniel were leaving, Bobby assured them he would take care of the blood work.

After all the goodbyes and watching Paula and Daniel drive away, Bobby couldn't help noticing his dad was looking a little perplexed. "Everything okay, Dad?"

"Oh yeah, I'm fine, son. I'm just curious about Daniel."

"Why, what's there to be curious about?"

"Well, the name Lombardo rings a bell, but I can't for the life of me remember why."

The very next day, Bobby made the appointments for the blood work. They were all eager to help and praying that one of them would be a match. Having contacted Janet the night before with Paula's news, she became a bit upset that she hadn't been there; she didn't hesitate to be a donor. She said she would get in touch with Ruth right away.

The next few days seemed to take forever, even though the hospital staff said they would put a rush on it. Bobby was in his office when he received the brown envelope with the return address of Massachusetts General Hospital. He knew he couldn't wait another second. To say he was surprised after reading the results of the donor match would be an understatement; he could only hope this would go well… for everyone.

CHAPTER TWELVE

Kathy couldn't help feeling concerned about Janet, especially after all she'd been through the last few months: losing her mum, finding out she wasn't her mum, and that her Aunt Ruth is her biological mother; then the daughter she gave up for adoption turned up a few days after the funeral, and now this. *I don't know where she gets her strength. I don't think I could handle all that.* Kathy couldn't keep from thinking about her own life: raised as a foster child, being placed in one home after the other. She never wanted to talk about her childhood; it was too painful, and the abuse she suffered from her foster parents was better left in the past. She would always think, "I'm so glad I never had kids or a man in my life. I'm just fine with my life the way it is, having Janet as a best friend and roommate." She knew she couldn't be happier or more content.

It was getting a little late, and Kathy wondered what was keeping Janet. She then heard the key in the door. "Janet, you're home. I was thinking we should go out for dinner, my treat."

"Oh, Kathy, that sounds so good, but I'm not sure I could eat anything."

"Oh, are you okay?"

"Well, yes, and no. Oh, Kathy, my head is all over the

place. Just before I left the office, I had a call from Bobby. He was calling to tell me they had a match for Paula."

"Oh, that's wonderful news. You don't look too happy though, Janet, what's wrong?"

"Kathy, it's Jane. Jane is a match, the only match. I don't know how she will respond to this. I can't help feeling guilty. I put her through so much when we were growing up, and now for her to be the only one who's a match, to donate one of her kidneys, to mine and Bobby's daughter."

"Janet, I'm sure she will be okay with this. She did offer, and was willing to get tested."

"Yes, you're right. She must have wanted to help; otherwise, she wouldn't have gotten tested. Oh, Kathy, I don't know what I would do without you. You always know just what to say when I'm upset. Let's go out for dinner, my treat."

At the same time, back in New England, Bobby was just turning into his driveway and praying Jane would be okay with what he was about to tell her.

Entering the front door, Bobby could smell supper cooking. "Hi Jane, I'm home, something smells good."

"Oh, Bobby, you're home. Supper is ready, so come and sit before it gets cold."

All through the meal, Jane couldn't help but notice Bobby's demeanour. "Bobby, you seem a little distracted. Did something happen at work today?"

"No, Jane, nothing like that. Come and join me in the living room; we need to talk. I received the paperwork today with the results of the donor match for Paula."

"Oh my… that didn't take long. Just let me get the dishes out of the way first."

"No, Jane, the dishes can wait!"

After sitting down, Jane looked at Bobby and said, "Oh, Bobby, it's you, isn't it? You're the match?"

"No, Jane, it's not me… it's you."

"What! Really? That's surprising. I thought for sure it would be you or Janet?"

"It doesn't work that way; parents are only a half-match, but an aunt can share a portion of their genes with the recipient, which can lead to better compatibility. However, there will be extensive medical testing required to ensure a suitable match."

"Okay, we'll just wait and see what happens."

"Jane, are you sure you're okay with this? You can refuse, you know, no one would think less of you for saying no."

"I guess I'm more surprised than anything. I really thought the odds of me being a match would have been very slim."

"Yes, you would think that would be the case, but donor matches can come from complete strangers as well. It's just the way it is. Again, Jane, we'll see what happens with more testing."

"How much time do we have, Bobby?"

"Not a lot. I should hear from Paula's doctor soon. I sent a message to him to contact me when he needed to do the surgery."

"Oh, Bobby, I think I need to think about this some more. I'm going to tidy up the kitchen and call it a night. I think you should, too. It's been a long day."

Jane couldn't sleep. Her mind was racing with so many thoughts, some going back to those days when she and Janet were in their teens. *No point in digging up the past*, she thought. She also decided there was only one way to get through this. After making her decision, Jane fell fast asleep. When she woke in the morning, she was surprised to find Bobby was gone. She was hoping to tell him about her decision. Jane couldn't help feeling relieved to have the day off to just relax and wait for the hospital to call about the final testing.

Sitting down with a cup of tea, Jane's thoughts turned to her mum. Oh, how she wished she were here. Her mum always knew just what to say to guide her on the right path. She felt her mum would be pleased with her decision.

After researching the medical facts and learning the surgery could be favourable for both her and Paula, she decided she would call Paula herself and give her the news that she would be her kidney donor.

CHAPTER THIRTEEN

The next morning, while packing her suitcase, Jane found herself feeling elated due to the fact that she was Paula's donor match. It was as if Paula would then be a part of her, granting them a bond that otherwise may never have happened.

"I'm all ready to go, Bobby; let's hit the road."

Driving down the highway, Bobby couldn't help but notice how relaxed Jane was. "Jane, you seem very upbeat, considering what lies ahead."

"Well, Bobby, the more I thought about it, the more I wanted to be Paula's kidney donor. It's hard to explain, but it just feels right."

"Jane, I couldn't be prouder of you, and so are Mum and Dad, and of course Liam too."

"Bobby, have you heard if Janet will be there after the surgery?"

"Yes, your dad mentioned that she was planning to be there."

"Oh, that's good, I'm sure it would mean a lot to Paula to have Janet there."

Arriving at the hospital, Jane looked over at Bobby. "You don't need to come in, Bobby. It will be a couple of days of testing before they can do the surgery, and as soon as I get the word, I'll call you."

"I'm coming in, Jane. I want to know what room you'll be in, and I also want to see Paula. Again, Jane, I can't tell you how proud I am of you. This is a huge gift you're giving her, not many would offer to do what you're doing."

"Bobby, I'm happy to be doing it. I just pray everything goes well."

After Jane was settled in her hospital room, and Bobby had a visit with Paula, he decided to make the short trip home. "Make sure you call me, Jane, as soon as you hear from the surgeon."

"Don't worry, Bobby, I will, and then you can let the others know."

The second day after being in the hospital, Jane and Paula had a visit from the surgeon, informing them that all went well with the testing and the surgery was scheduled for tomorrow morning. He explained the surgery and what they could expect following the transplant, leaving them confident that all would be well.

Jane immediately called Bobby, who told her he would be there in the morning, and he would bring his mum and dad, and that Liam said he would call Janet to let her know.

The next morning, they all sat together in the waiting room, hoping for good news of the surgery, which was still taking place after three hours. Bobby's dad spoke up, saying, "I thought they said three hours; it's almost four."

"Dad, I'm sure we'll hear soon. We just have to be patient." Bobby had to admit he, too, was a little anxious; he just had to stay calm for everyone's sake.

Bobby noticed his mum and dad, and Liam, were looking tired. "Why don't you three take a break, go down to the cafeteria for a coffee. Daniel and I will be here, and as soon as we hear anything, we'll let you know."

After settling in at the cafeteria, Bobby's dad looked at Liam and asked, "So, Liam, what are your thoughts regarding Daniel?"

"He seems like a decent young man. He's well educated, professional, comes from a good background."

"Are you sure about that, the background I mean. You're not familiar with the name Lombardo, are you?"

"No, I guess not. Why? Is there something I should know?"

"Well, the name sounded familiar to me when I first met him, but I couldn't remember why. I then got to thinking, maybe it was connected to something when I was still working on the police force. I then decided to make a call to one of my buddies on the force, and sure enough, he remembered. We were on a case years ago, and it involved some Mafia members." The look on Liam's face said it all. "Yes, you guessed it—their name was Lombardo!!"

"Were they caught?" Liam asked.

"Some were, and some of them got away with it. I just don't like our granddaughter being mixed up with the likes of them.

"Oh, I agree, one hundred percent. I think Bobby should know about this."

"Absolutely, but I think we should put this on hold for now, don't you?"

Bobby's mum spoke up, "You two are imagining things. I think Daniel is a fine young man. I don't think you should be gossiping about something that has nothing to do with him. I think we should go back and find out how the girls are doing."

It was a long three hours, but the doctor finally appeared, assuring them that everything went well with the transplant and that they could see them soon.

CHAPTER FOURTEEN

Kathy couldn't help thinking of Janet and how her sister and daughter were doing after the transplant surgery. She sometimes wondered what it would be like to have a child. She came close, but it was a blessing that it never happened. Oh, how she wished she could erase it all from her mind, but she couldn't, no matter how hard she tried; it was a long time ago, twenty years, yet it still felt like yesterday. She was seventeen, and still in foster care, but with graduation just a week away, she could soon put this all behind her. She planned on getting a job and a place of her own, maybe finding a roommate or two to help with expenses. She thought, "No way am I staying here any longer. I'll be eighteen in a few days, and I can walk away from foster care for good." She remembered trying on her prom dress just to make sure everything was perfect. Then, as she was taking it off, the bedroom door opened, and there he was (foster dad). She'd never forget that voice: "Well, well, what have we here?"

Kathy froze; she never liked him, especially when he looked her up and down with a smirk on his face. She tried to keep her distance, and not having any proof, there was no point in reporting it. The way she felt, they probably wouldn't believe her even if she had proof. The memory was so clear of him closing the bedroom door, her grabbing her robe to cover herself when he reached and pulled the robe out of her hands.

The next thing she remembered was lying on her bed naked, and as he was going out the door, he turned and warned her, "If you tell anyone about this, you'll regret it. Oh, and no one would believe you anyway, you're just a foster kid." Kathy could still hear those words, no matter how hard she tried to forget.

After graduation and turning eighteen, Kathy said goodbye to Boston and good riddance to foster care. She and a friend set off for New York City and started a new life. She would be forever grateful to God that she never became pregnant. She just wished it wouldn't haunt her. *Maybe I could confide in Janet; I'm sure she would listen and maybe help me put this away for good.*

Sitting there, Kathy began to wonder how different her life would have been if the right one had come along and they had married and had children. Her thoughts then drifted to her background: where did she come from, who were her parents, and did she have siblings? The more she thought about it, the more curious she became. She then heard the phone ringing. She jumped up to answer it, hoping it was Janet with good news. "Hello."

"Hi Kathy, it's me, Janet. I have good news: the transplant went very well. The doctor told us he was very pleased and that Jane was the perfect match. Paula's new kidney started working immediately, which is a very good sign."

"Oh, Janet, that's wonderful! I'm so happy for you and

your family."

"Thank you, Kathy. I should be home soon. Paula and Jane have lots of support, and I've taken enough time from work. I don't want Macy's to think I'm taking advantage."

"I don't think you have to worry about that, but it will be nice to have you home again."

"Okay, Kathy, see you soon."

Kathy felt so much better after talking to Janet. Janet felt like family, family that she never had. From the first time they met, something just clicked, and when Janet became her roommate, it was like it was meant to be. She couldn't wait for her to come home.

CHAPTER FIFTEEN

They all sat in the waiting room once again, hoping any second, they would get the "okay" to see Janet and Paula in their rooms. Just then, a nurse started walking towards them. She was smiling. Bobby assumed that had to be a good sign.

The nurse, still smiling and making eye contact with each and every one of them, proclaimed that the girls were doing well and that they could receive visitors. She explained it was best if only one person visited at a time, and she advised keeping the visit short.

Being the husband and father, Bobby jumped up, then turned to Janet.

"It's okay, Bobby, go ahead. I can wait a few minutes."

"Thank you, Janet. I promise I won't stay long."

Fortunately, the girls were sharing a room. Bobby immediately rushed to Jane's bedside. "Oh, Jane, how are you feeling? The doctor told us everything went well for both you and Paula."

"I'm fine, Bobby, we're both in good hands here, and I'll be back home in no time."

"This is all such a relief," Bobby said. Then, turning to Paula, he asked, "How are you feeling, after all you've been through?"

"I'm okay. I guess I'll know more when the drugs wear off. I'm just so very, very grateful to Jane for being so selfless. She not only saved me from having to endure dialysis, she gave me a new life, for which I will always be grateful." She then turned her head towards Jane, and with tears in her eyes, she said, "I love you, Jane."

Jane, hearing this, also reacted with emotion. "Oh, Paula, I love you too, and I'm so happy that I was your donor match."

Bobby was also tearing up. "Well, girls, I'm going to leave you to it. Janet is patiently waiting to see you both." After giving them both hugs, Bobby left, telling them he would be back the next day.

After everyone had spent a few minutes with Jane and Paula, the nurse came back, telling them the girls needed to rest.

Driving home, Bobby, his parents, and Liam were so relieved that the surgeries went as well as they did. Bobby's dad spoke up, "Well, Bobby, now that that's over, and we can move on, something is weighing on my mind that I need to talk to you about."

Bobby's mum, sounding annoyed, stated, "Bobby doesn't need to hear any of that foolishness; the girls are barely out of surgery, and you're bringing that up again!"

Bobby looked in the rearview mirror at his mother. "Mum, what are you so upset about?"

"It's nothing for you to worry about, Bobby. Your father is playing detective again, and I don't like it. He needs to keep his nose out of other people's business."

"What's this about, Dad?"

"Oh, nothing, son, we can maybe talk about it another time."

"Okay, if you're sure."

"Yeah, I'm sure."

Bobby could hear his mum whispering in the back seat with his dad, and then all was quiet. Arriving back home in Chelmsford, Bobby dropped off his parents and Liam; he just wanted to go home for some quiet time. Entering the house, he practically fell into the chair. He was exhausted, but in a good way. He was so thankful that everything went as well as it did. Now, if only his dad would keep his nose out of Daniel's background. God only knows what he's up to. Bobby did know one thing, and that was that his father would never give up on something he felt wasn't right. Thinking out loud, he said, "I'm going to have to keep an eye on you, Dad."

CHAPTER SIXTEEN

Unlocking the apartment door, Janet called out, "I'm home, Kathy."

Kathy, feeling relieved, answered, "Great to have you home again. It's so quiet here when you're gone." She hugged Kathy and then headed to the kitchen, saying, "I'll make some tea."

"That would be lovely, but first I have to give Ruth a call. I promised her I would let her know when I got home."

Kathy was looking forward to sitting down with Janet. She wasn't sure when she would bring up her past or if she ever could, especially after all Janet had been through the past couple of months.

Janet entered the living room with a big smile, saying, "Oh my, I'm so thankful that's over and that it all went well. Oh, Kathy, this is lovely! It's so nice to just sit with my friend over a cup of tea."

They sat quietly, saying very little. Janet looked over at Kathy, saying, "Kathy, you're very quiet. Everything okay at work?"

"Oh yeah, work's fine. I'm just a little tired, I guess. I haven't been sleeping well."

"Oh, what's keeping you up? Do you want to talk about

it? You know you can tell me anything… Kathy, you never talk about your family. Do you still have family in Boston?"

"Oh, Janet, I don't want to burden you with my story. You have enough on your plate as it is."

"Kathy, I'm not just your roommate, I'm your friend, and I'd be happy to listen to whatever it is that's on your mind."

"Thank you, that means so much. The thing is, I've never talked to anyone about my growing-up years. I've kept it buried all this time, and I'm afraid of what will happen if I dig it up."

"I'm so sorry, Kathy. What about your parents or siblings? Can you reach out to them?"

"Oh, Janet, I don't remember my parents. I don't even know who they are. I was placed in foster care at a very young age. I don't remember anything before that."

"Kathy, I'm so sorry to hear that. I hope you had good foster parents?

"Some were good, and some weren't."

Janet instinctively knew there was something Kathy was keeping to herself, and for God knew how long.

"Kathy, if you need to talk to someone, I'm here, or maybe a therapist could help. It's always good to talk to someone; you need to unburden yourself from whatever this is."

Kathy broke down, tears running down her face. She looked up at Janet and said, "Janet, I wouldn't know where to begin. I've kept it buried all these years, but for some reason it's come back to haunt me." Tears turned to sobs, and then, gasping for air, she whispered, "I don't know… what to do."

Janet immediately got up and wrapped her arms around Kathy, trying to console her, assuring her it would be okay. She told Kathy, "You know I'll always be there, ready to listen."

Kathy, crying uncontrollably, exclaimed between sobs, "He told me no one would ever believe a foster kid!"

"Oh my God, Kathy, what happened to you? Who did this?"

"It was my last foster home, I was so excited about graduating, and prom night. I was in my bedroom trying on my prom dress when he came home early. I was taking off my dress when he came into my room. I grabbed my robe to cover myself, but he was too quick. He grabbed the robe away from me and threw it on the floor. I tried to stop him, Janet, I tried, but he was too strong… He raped me… he and then he laughed and said, 'Don't even think about telling anyone; no one is going to believe a foster kid.' The next week, I graduated and I turned eighteen, so I no longer had to stay in the system. That's when I moved to New York."

"Kathy, I'm so, so sorry for what you've been through. I really think you should talk to a professional about this, and also you should report him to the police. Only God knows how many other children he's abused."

That night, as Janet lay in her bed, she couldn't stop thinking about Kathy and the life she endured growing up. Her thoughts then turned to her own childhood, and just how fortunate she was to have her parents and sister, who always loved her, in spite of all she put them through. At that moment, she made a vow to help Kathy.

The next morning, she prepared breakfast for her and Kathy. Later, over coffee, she approached the subject to Kathy about going to the police. "Kathy, you need to go to the police to report what happened to you. You could also check with the Child Welfare System. They could look into your background and maybe find your family."

Kathy was reluctant at first. "I'm not sure I could do that, Janet. It's been a long time, and yes, you're right, it should be reported. I've always thought that no one would believe me… but I'm not that young girl anymore. As for the Child Welfare System, I have to admit, I've thought about looking into my background, but I'm not sure."

"Oh, Kathy, I really think you should. You just never know, you might have a sister or brother out there, and maybe they have been trying to find you."

"Wow, I never thought of that. You could be right, Janet, but I don't think I could do this on my own, not any of it, especially going to the police and reporting that bastard!"

"Don't worry about that, Kathy, I'll be right beside you every step of the way."

The next day, Kathy made some enquiries into the Child Welfare System to see if they could help her. After explaining that she grew up in Boston, she was afraid they couldn't look into it. They assured her they would contact the Boston branch of Child Protective Services and that there would be an investigation regarding her case. They also explained that she would have to come to the office to lay a complaint. After booking the appointment, Kathy hung up the phone, and then a chill went down her spine. "Oh my God, this is really happening!"

It had been two weeks since Kathy and Janet had gone to the police and the Child Welfare System. It felt like yesterday, she was so nervous, she couldn't stop shaking while sitting in the waiting area, afraid they wouldn't believe her story. They believed everything, and they told her they would look into it as soon as possible, explaining that this is one of many abuse cases they are investigating. She could never have done this on her own. Janet was her rock, always there for her and never doubting her story.

CHAPTER SEVENTEEN

After being home from the hospital for a week, Jane was feeling quite well, physically and mentally. Just as she hoped, she and Paula had formed a bond during the time they spent together in the hospital. Being her kidney donor and sharing the same room had definitely brought them closer together. So much so that Jane found herself missing Paula; she was a lovely girl and very intelligent. She was sorry that Paula never had the chance to meet her grandmother. But then again, Bobby's mum was her grandmother and actually, Aunt Ruth would be her biological grandmother. *Oh, what a mixed-up family we have*, she thought, *and we still have some explaining to do. I wonder when Janet will tell Paula that Aunt Ruth is her grandmother. Soon, I hope, I'm tired of all these secrets. Then there's Bobby's dad, oh, the questions he was asking Paula about her background. Thankfully, Bobby stepped in and told him to stop.* Paula just smiled, saying, "Oh, it's okay, I don't mind, and I completely understand." Then he started questioning Bobby about Daniel's background, and again she thought she heard him use the term "mafia." She hoped she had heard wrong and put it all down to him being a retired police officer. She was looking forward to going back to work, and maybe when she was strong enough, she would have everyone there for dinner, oh, and Janet could bring her friend Kathy, whom she'd heard so much about.

"I'm home, Jane." Bobby came rushing into the living room. "Don't worry about supper, I brought us some take-out from mum's kitchen. She called me at work and asked me to pick it up. She was going to deliver it herself, but thought you might be resting; she didn't want to disturb you."

"Bobby, your parents are the best. That was so thoughtful of your mum and your dad, too. Bobby, speaking of your dad, what do you think about him asking so many questions about Paula and Daniel? Don't you think he goes a little too far?"

"Jane, you have to keep in mind that he was a police officer and was often assigned to detective work. He can't help being curious. After all, Paula and Daniel were complete strangers until Paula turned up on your parents' doorstep."

"Yeah, I suppose that makes sense. I just find it a little rude and intimidating for Paula and Daniel."

"Well, I could speak to him about it, ask him to tone it down with the questions."

"That would be good, because I'm planning to have a dinner party soon, so we can all get together. I also thought I would ask Janet to bring her roommate, Kathy, and they could travel with Aunt Ruth."

"Sounds like a great idea, Jane, but not until you're stronger."

CHAPTER EIGHTEEN

Bobby's dad sat quietly in his home office, which he refused to let go of after he retired. He missed being on the police force, but at his age, he knew he had no choice. But that won't stop him from being inquisitive. He just couldn't seem to get that name "Lombardo" out of his head. He knew what he would do. He would call his old partner Franky and see if he remembers the name.

After finding the number, he picked up the phone and dialed. Hearing Franky answer, he replied, "Hey Franky, Robert here… your old partner."

"Robert, how the hell are you? I haven't heard from you in ages."

"Oh, come on now, it hasn't been that long. What do you say we get together for a coffee, my treat?"

"Sure, sounds great. When do you want to meet up?"

"How's tomorrow morning sound?"

"Okay by me. Same old spot?"

"That's the one. Nine o'clock, okay?"

"Not a problem, see you there, buddy."

Entering the coffee shop, Robert looked for a table at the back where they could talk privately. Just as he was pulling out a chair to sit down, he saw Franky enter the shop. He waved him down to the back.

Franky was quick to extend his hand before sitting down. "Good to see you, buddy."

"Yeah, you too, Franky." After two cups of coffee and chatting about the BOSTON RED SOX, Franky looked Robert in the eye and asked, "Sooo, Robert, ole buddy, what's going on? Something tells me you need help with something?"

"Ahh, Franky, you know me too well, and yes, I do have a question for you. I also might need a favour."

"Spit it out, partner, I'll do what I can."

"Does the name 'Lombardo' ring a bell?"

"Yes, yes, it does. His name was Joe… Joe Lombardo. What's this about Robert? Why are you so interested in the Lombardo case?"

"Well, Franky, it's a long story. You see, way back when my son was in high school, he got his girlfriend's sister pregnant. Yeah, I know what you're thinking, but it wasn't like that. He was drunk at a graduation party. Anyway, her parents sent her away to a home for unwed mothers, where she gave the baby up for adoption. As it turns out, the baby, who is now twenty-three, showed up a few months ago, looking for her biological family. She needed a kidney transplant. The match turned out to be Bobby's wife Jane, sister to the biological mother."

"Wow, that's quite the story. So, you're telling me you have a granddaughter."

"You got it. But the thing is, she's engaged, and her fiancé's name is… Daniel Lombardo, from Boston."

"Buddy, are you kidding me?"

"I wish I were, but no, this is the God's honest truth. I've met them both; she's a nurse, and he's a lawyer. He says he works with the family business. Seems like a stand-up guy, but it's the name that's got me worried."

"What about your son Bobby? This is his daughter, isn't he or the rest of the family concerned?"

"No, you see, they're not familiar with the name Lombardo, but I recognized it right away. I just couldn't remember why, and the wife wants me to leave it alone, but I can't. So, Franky, that's why I called you. I thought maybe between the two of us, we could find out if the Lombardos are still mixed up in organized crime. What do you think?"

"Yeah, sure, anything for my ole partner. I don't have anything else to do."

"Oh, that's great, Franky. Where do you think we could find some information on this?"

"I'm not sure, but I still have some connections on the force. Actually, there is a guy I can ask to do a little research, and as soon as I find out anything, I'll get back to you."

After a strong handshake and a pat on the back, they left

the coffee shop.

Arriving home, Robert heard his wife calling out to him. "Robert, where have you been? You've been gone for hours."

"Oh, my old buddy, Franky, and I met up for a coffee, thought it would be nice to see him. After all, we were partners on the force for years."

"Okay, and what did you two talk about?"

"Oh, you know, just the usual stuff, the weather, politics, and mostly about the Red Sox and how they should look for a new coach."

"Really, nothing else?"

"No, what else would there be?"

"I can think of a thing or two. Robert, I know you, and I know how you think. Once a detective, always a detective. I want you to promise me you won't go digging up anything about Daniel or Paula."

The next day, Bobby received a call from his mom. As soon as Bobby answered the phone and heard his mother's voice, he knew something was up. "Mum, slow down, what's this about?"

"I'm sorry, Bobby, it's about your dad. I'm afraid he's up to something."

"What do you mean, Mum? What could he be up to?"

"You must remember him asking Daniel all those

questions. I don't like it, and he needs to stop. I think you should say something to him. Something else, too, I thought was a little odd."

"Oh, what was that?"

"Well, he was gone for hours this morning, told me he went for coffee with his friend Franky from the police force. Now he hasn't seen Franky since he retired, so why now? I'm sure he's up to something. He did say he was familiar with the name Lombardo, and I'm thinking he's looking into the background. You know your father, once he gets an idea, there's no stopping him.

"Okay, Mum, don't worry, I'll have a word with him, and hopefully put a stop to this."

"That sounds good, just make sure he listens."

"Yes, Mum, I'll do my best. Gotta go, talk later."

"Bye, Son."

It had been a few days since Robert met with Franky in the coffee shop, and there was no word from Franky yet. He didn't want to call him, but he wasn't sure how much longer he could wait. Being home alone, he was hoping he would call before his wife came home. Just as he sat down to read the morning paper, the phone rang. "Oh, I hope that's Franky." He answered the call, "Hello… hey Franky, I was hoping that was you. Did you find out anything on the Lombardo case?"

"Yeah, actually, I did. How about we get together for

coffee, and I can tell you what I've got so far."

"Sounds good to me, buddy, just say when?"

"How about now? I'll meet you there."

"I'm on my way."

Just as he was going out the front door, Bobby pulled into the driveway. "Hey Dad, where are you off to this early? I thought you and I could grab a coffee this morning."

"Oh, sorry, son, but I have a doctor's appointment. Maybe another time, gotta run."

"Okay, Dad, but make it soon." Bobby stood in the driveway watching his dad fly down the street. Thinking to himself, hopefully, he won't get caught speeding.

Robert arrived at the coffee shop to find Franky sitting in their old spot at the back.

"Just like old times, eh, Robert?"

"Yeah, kind of."

"What's up, buddy? You look a little upset?"

"Wouldn't you know it, just as I was leaving, Bobby showed up, wanting to take me for a coffee. I lied and told him I had a doctor's appointment.

"Maybe you should have brought him with you. I have something I think you both will be interested in."

"Really, what did you find out about the Lombardos?"

"Oh, man, there's a lot to tell. Starting with Joe Lombardo, also known as 'Big Joe.' He was charged with racketeering and eighteen murders, along with some other gangsters. Big Joe was born in Sicily, then moved to New York at age eleven. The family then moved to Boston. He was well respected in the Mafia. Later, he was charged, but the Grand Jury sitting in Boston later freed him and two others in a murder case. He died of natural causes in 1969."

"So, the question is, how do I find out if he's connected to Daniel?"

"Well, you could come right out and ask him, but you probably don't want to do that. So why don't I see what else I can find? Maybe do some more digging into the Lombardo family tree?"

"Okay, let's do some more digging. I want to be sure before I say anything to Bobby or the rest of them."

"I can do that, buddy, no problem. Just leave it with me."

"Thanks, Franky, I really appreciate you doing this."

"Anything for my ole partner, and I'll be in touch as soon as I have more info."

"Thanks again, Franky. This is a big help." As Robert left the coffee shop, he hoped it would be good news and that Daniel had no connection to that bunch.

CHAPTER NINETEEN

Jane, feeling completely recovered from the surgery, sat down on her front porch with a cup of coffee. She couldn't help feeling grateful for how well everything worked out. She then noticed there was a definite chill in the air. Summer was gone, and the fall was fast approaching. Thanksgiving being just around the corner, she thought it would be the perfect time to have the dinner party. Therefore, she had some planning to do and phone calls to make. Her last call was to Janet. The phone was ringing, but no answer. Just as she was about to hang up, Janet answered, "Hello."

"Hi Janet, so glad I caught you."

"Hi Jane, so nice to hear from you. How are you?"

"I'm doing well, Janet, and I have something to tell you. I'm planning to have a dinner party on Thanksgiving for the family. I also thought it would be nice if you brought Kathy, your roommate. It would be lovely to meet her, and you could travel together with Aunt Ruth. What do you think?"

"Jane, it sounds lovely, but are you sure you're feeling up to it?"

"Oh yes, absolutely, and Dad is looking forward to having you and Kathy and Aunt Ruth stay with him."

"All sounds good, I'll check in with Ruth about travel

arrangements, and I'm sure Kathy will be delighted to come. Thanksgiving sounds like the perfect time, can't wait to see everyone. Oh, and thanks, Jane, for thinking of Kathy."

"Janet, it will be my pleasure, and Paula and Daniel are also looking forward to seeing everyone."

"Jane, thank you again for doing this. I'm sure it will mean a lot to Paula as well."

After good-byes and hanging up the phone, Jane couldn't help noticing how much her sister had changed since their mum died. "All for the good, Mum, just wish you were here to see it, but then again, maybe you can."

CHAPTER TWENTY

Kathy knew her decision to take a leave of absence from work was the right thing to do. Her anxiety level was through the roof; she couldn't help wondering, *maybe I shouldn't have gone down that old road.* Then again, she knew Janet was right in telling her to report what happened all those years ago. She did have to admit that because of her talk with the counselor, she did feel some of the weight was lifted. She thought to herself, "I just wish I could hear from the Child Welfare System so that I can get this over with."

She was so grateful that Janet came into her life. She never had anyone whom she felt close to or that she could trust. Being a foster child, always moving from one place to another, it was impossible to bond with anyone. Kathy then decided she would surprise Janet with supper when she came home from work.

Janet couldn't wait to get home and tell Kathy about her call from Jane. She couldn't help feeling concerned about Kathy; hopefully, this will all go well. Arriving home and unlocking the apartment door, Janet called out to Kathy, "Something smells good… can't wait, I'm starving. Kathy, I have news: Jane called me at work to tell me she is having Thanksgiving dinner at her house, and you're invited. Please say yes?"

"Janet, that sounds lovely. Yes, I would love that, and it would be so nice to meet your family."

"Perfect, I'll let Jane know. Oh, and we'll be travelling with Ruth, so no need to worry about transportation."

"I'll have to find something to wear."

"I'm sure we can find something at work. Macy's just received their fall inventory; we should go shopping this weekend."

"Yes, that sounds like fun. I'd love that. Now let's eat before it gets cold."

While sitting down at the table, Janet couldn't hold back from questioning Kathy about her situation.

"Kathy, I'm assuming you haven't heard back from the Child Welfare System?"

"No, nothing yet, but she did say they had plenty of cases they are currently working on. So it's probably going to take a while."

"Well, why don't you just try to relax and concentrate on getting ready for the big dinner. Now, there is something I want to warn you about; Bobby's mum and dad will be there, and Bobby's dad, Robert, is the type who is always asking people questions about their background. He doesn't mean any harm. I think he's just curious. Being a retired police officer, I don't think he can help himself.

"Well, I couldn't tell him anything anyway, because I

know nothing about my background. Only that my last name is O'Brien."

"Kathy, have you thought any more about searching for your biological family?"

"Actually, I have. I'm just anxious about going there."

"You'll know when the time is right; these things have a way of letting you know when that is."

Lying in bed that night, Kathy found it impossible to fall asleep. She was overwhelmed with trying to remember her childhood. *If only I could remember something, anything that would give me a connection to someone.* The earliest memory she had was being in a foster home around the age of three or four. It was Christmas, and she was sitting in front of a Christmas tree with three other children. A lady was taking their picture, but she couldn't see her face in the camera. After that, it was one foster home after the other. Then, in that moment, she knew it was time; tomorrow, she would contact the Foster Care System and ask if they had her birth certificate on record. With a feeling of hope in her heart, she closed her eyes and slept.

CHAPTER TWENTY-ONE

Robert was getting a little impatient waiting to hear back from Franky. Maybe I could have done this on my own, but then again, Franky still has contacts on the inside. I guess I'll just have to wait and see.

Another week went by, and he just couldn't wait any longer. He picked up the phone and called Franky, who picked up on the first ring.

"Hey, Robert, I knew that was you."

"Yeah, Franky, just wondering how you're making out. Did you find any connection to the Lombardo name?"

"Well, how about if we meet up again. I'm not comfortable talking about this over the phone."

"Okay by me. Wanna meet now?"

"Yeah, now fine."

"On my way."

Robert couldn't help feeling excited. He also felt guilty going behind his wife's back, and the trouble he'd be in if she found out. But then again, he didn't care. As far as he was concerned, these things needed to be uncovered, the truth needed to be revealed.

As he entered the coffee shop, there was Franky, waiting

for him with two cups of coffee sitting on the table.

"Take a seat, Robert. I got you a coffee."

"Thanks, bud, so what's up? Tell me you found something."

"Well, yeah, I found something, but it's not what you think."

"What's that supposed to mean?"

"Well, Robert, this Daniel Lombardo that you're so concerned about isn't really connected to Joe Lombardo or Big Joe, whatever you want to call him."

"So, what exactly do you mean by 'not really connected'?"

"They are connected by blood, but very distant. Daniel's immediate family has always been on the right side of the law. While I was searching, though, something else popped up when I was going through the old records."

"Wow, that's a relief. I was a little nervous about the mafia connection. I guess I can put that to rest. So, what popped up, Franky? Tell me!"

"Well, it appears that about thirty-some years ago, Daniel's dad got a young girl pregnant, and from what I could tell, he was engaged to someone else at the same time. The parents would never have approved of the one he got pregnant, referring to her as low-class. So he ended the relationship. Apparently, she gave birth to a baby girl and tried to raise her on her own. With little or no help from her father, she turned to prostitution and drugs. They thought someone in her building called the police when she overdosed on drugs. Then the Child Welfare System stepped in and placed the little one in foster care.”

“Holy cow, Franky, that’s quite the story, but I have to say, I’m relieved there’s no connection to that Joe Lombardo. So, this little girl is out there somewhere, well, she’s not a little girl now, she must be well into her thirties. Oh yeah… and she would be a half-sister to Daniel. Now, one more question: Did the records state the mother’s name?”

“Yes, I saw the mother’s name was ‘Mary O’Brien.’”

CHAPTER TWENTY-TWO

Upon entering the huge brick building, Kathy made her way to the office of the Child Foster Care System. Taking a seat in the waiting area, she couldn't help wondering about all the little children whose lives depended on this very place. She also couldn't help feeling emotional; never having a mother's love and protection, or a dad she could depend on, she was finding it hard to hold back the tears. *Then again*, she thought, *when they search my background, there will be names and maybe, just maybe, I'll find out who my parents are, and where they are, if they're still alive.*

At that moment, the office door opened, and a lady introduced herself, "My name is Winifred, and you must be Kathy; you may come in now." After entering the office and taking a seat opposite the lady's desk, Kathy tried her best to remain calm.

"So, Kathy, how can I help?"

"I'm hoping you can find something in my records that will state who my birth parents are. I have no memory of either of them. My earliest memory was being in Foster Care, I was probably three or four. I remember sitting in front of a Christmas tree with three other children, and a lady was taking our picture. I can't remember the lady's name, or even what she looked like, just that she was holding the camera and telling us to smile. There were so many other foster homes, all just a blur, except for the last one, which I'm sure you've been made aware of.

"Kathy, I'm so sorry that happened to you, and I want to reassure you, it is being thoroughly investigated as we speak. Now, about finding your biological family, the information we have is your last name being O'Brien, and your birth date was 2nd April, 1951. Now that's a while ago, so it may take a little longer, but the information is definitely in storage, and I will do my very best to find it, and as soon as I do, I will call you."

"That sounds very encouraging. Thank you so much."

As Kathy made her way home on the subway, she couldn't help feeling hopeful; she had a strong feeling this would lead to something positive. Arriving home, the excitement was growing; she couldn't wait to meet her biological family. Her thoughts then turned to all those foster children she'd known, wondering if they, too, were searching for blood relatives. It was hard to watch them come and go, never knowing what the circumstances would be. She recalled back to when she was little, and being afraid of strangers, not knowing what to expect. "Oh, I pray I get a call soon, but I can't sit around here waiting for the phone to ring. I guess it's time I went back to work."

Janet couldn't wait to find out how Kathy made out at her appointment with foster care. As soon as she came through the door, she asked, "How did it go at the foster care office? Were they able to give you any information regarding your biological family?"

"Not exactly, Janet, but I am hopeful. The lady told me she was going to do everything she could to find them. So I just have to wait and try to be patient."

"I would say you're probably one of many who are looking for family."

Going back to work did make a difference, but Kathy still hadn't heard from foster care, and it had been over two weeks since she contacted them about finding her biological family. Janet was such a good friend, always trying to cheer her up and telling her how these things take time, especially allowing for the fact that it took place in Boston, not New York City.

Kathy was looking forward to meeting Janet's family. From what Janet had told her, that family certainly had some issues, but they seemed to be doing fine now, and she was happy for Janet.

Daniel wished he had his own place, but his parents kept insisting he should stay at home and save his money, especially since he and Paula were now engaged to be married. The only problem he had with living at home was having to listen to his parents arguing. Lately, it seemed to be getting more frequent. It was hard to make out exactly what they would be saying, being in their bedroom behind closed doors, until one night he came in through the back door. They never heard him come in, probably due to all the shouting. Standing quietly in the kitchen, trying to make out what the shouting was about, he heard his mother refer to "that RIFRAFF, Mary O'Brien." He then heard his dad mention the word daughter who was probably placed in foster care due to the mother being deceased. Becoming upset, he told Daniel's mother she was being insensitive, and that he had the right to find his daughter.

Daniel was in shock; he couldn't believe that after all these years, nothing was ever said about this. Then again, knowing his mother and how she put herself above everyone else, she would never want this to come out. Daniel couldn't hold back. Walking into the living room, he confronted his parents, "Mum, Dad, what is going on?! What's this about a daughter? Do I have a sister I don't know about?"

Daniel's mum spoke in a sarcastic tone, "Ever since Paula

found out about her adoption, your father has gone back to a time before we were married, a time that should stay in the past. I have nothing more to say. I'm going to bed."

Daniel turned to his dad, asking, "Dad, is this true? Do I have a sister?"

"Oh, Daniel, it's a long story, one I'm not proud of. I cheated on your mother when we were engaged. I'd known Mary for years. Actually, we grew up in the same neighbourhood. I just happened to be out one night with a buddy of mine, and I bumped into Mary at a bar. She was going through a hard time, and I guess I felt sorry for her. She invited me back to her apartment, and I'm sure you can figure out what happened after that. I offered to help financially when she told me she was pregnant, but I couldn't do any more as I was engaged to your mother. I continued to help Mary until your mother found out about it. Later on, I learned through a mutual friend of Mary's that she had become addicted to drugs and overdosed. She was taken to the hospital, but she didn't survive. I then learned that the baby was placed in the Foster Care System. I just let it go, thinking she would be better off; there was nothing I could do. Your mother forbade me from ever mentioning it again. So you see, when Paula found out she was adopted, it got me thinking; my daughter is out there somewhere, and she too has the right to know who her biological family is. So the answer to your question is, yes, you do have a sister."

Daniel couldn't get over the fact that he had a sister or

half-sister; it made no difference. Growing up as an only child, he always wished for a baby brother or sister. He tried to figure out how old she would be, considering his parents had been married a while before he was born. After doing the math, he thought, "She has to be in her thirties."

Daniel couldn't get past the fact that he had a half-sister. So what to do? He knew that very moment that he had to look into this, not just for himself, but also for his dad. After telling Paula his dad's story, she totally agreed that he should make some inquiries with the Foster Care System. "My God, Daniel, she could be out there looking for her biological family, just as I was. Daniel, you're a lawyer, couldn't you look into this?"

"Funny you should say that. I just happened to be at the office of the Foster Care System the other day, looking into a case concerning a foster child. I thought to myself, how difficult this must be for the people who grew up in foster care, not to mention the abuse some of them suffered. Now, they're searching for family. I'm sure you've heard stories, being a nurse. You must see children from foster homes more often than you'd like.

"Oh, Paula, I don't like going behind my parents' backs, especially my mother. You know how she is; she would never want anything that might bring shame to the family. She would be furious if she knew I was looking into it."

"Well, she doesn't need to know. You could be working

on a case for the Law Firm, just like the one you were working on the other day. You and your dad could do this together, and again, your mother doesn't need to know. Then again, she might have to learn to accept what is."

CHAPTER TWENTY-FOUR

It was a beautiful morning, even with a chill in the air, as Kathy and Janet made their way to work at Macy's. So much hustle and bustle, but they both loved the atmosphere of New York City. Kathy always enjoyed the walk, but today she found it hard to take her mind off her troubles—still no word from Foster Care. *Surely any day now*, she thought.

Janet gave Kathy a poke in the arm. "Kathy, did you hear what I said? You're a million miles away."

"Sorry, Janet, I was just thinking about when I'll hear from Winifred, the lady at the Foster Care Office."

"Oh, yes, of course, I'm sorry, I didn't mean to be insensitive. I was just saying that Thanksgiving is just around the corner, and I can't wait for you to meet everyone."

"Yes, me too, I'm so looking forward to being with a real family at Thanksgiving. I actually have something to be thankful for."

"I feel the same way, Kathy. Having you and Paula come into my life has definitely made me see things from a different perspective."

Entering Macy's, they were surprised to find it so busy, but then again, Thanksgiving was just around the corner. As Kathy was opening the office door, she could hear her phone ringing. *Who would be calling this early?* she thought, *it probably has something to do with the latest order.*

"Hello, MACY'S DEPARTMENT STORE, Kathy O'Brien speaking."

"Hi Kathy, Winifred here from Foster Care. I'm wondering if you could come to the office later today, around four o'clock? I have your records here from the office in Boston from the time you entered the System."

"Yes, yes of course, I can do that. I'll see you at four o'clock."

Hanging up the phone, Kathy was shaking. *Oh my, this is really happening!* As hard as she tried to stay focused at work, it was next to impossible. During break time, she rushed over to Janet's office. She didn't bother to knock. Barging in, she went straight to Janet's desk. "Janet, she called this morning, Winifred, from Foster Care. She said she has my records from the Foster Care office in Boston."

"Oh, Kathy, that's great news! When will you see her?"

"I have an appointment today at four o'clock. I'd be so grateful if you could come with me?"

"Yes, of course, I should be finished here by then. We'll get a cab, so we won't be late."

Arriving at the office of the Foster Care System, Kathy was trying so hard to remain calm. Taking a seat in the waiting area, she couldn't help feeling grateful Janet was there by her side.

They didn't have to wait long; the door opened, and Winifred, with a smile on her face, said, "Come in, Kathy, and yes, you can bring your friend with you, if you wish. Please, take a seat. Kathy, I have good news concerning your biological father, but I'm sorry to say, your mother passed away due to a drug overdose, and died the same day you were placed in Foster Care."

"Who was my mother? What was her name?"

"Her name was Mary O'Brien. She was of Irish descent and lived in Boston, Massachusetts."

"And my father? Were they married?"

"No, Kathy, they weren't married."

"Well, did my father know what happened, or did he even care? Did he look for me when I was placed in foster care? Who is he, what's his name, please, tell me."

"Kathy, your father's name is Marco Lombardo, and he is currently living in Boston, Massachusetts."

Kathy immediately looked at Janet, who also looked surprised. Kathy couldn't help asking, "Are you sure his name is Lombardo? What does he do for a living?"

"He has an established Law Firm, it goes by the name of Lombardo Law."

"Oh, my God, I think I know who he is, or maybe it's just a coincidence. I don't know what to do now. What should I do?"

"Well, Kathy, that's entirely up to you. You could reach out to him at his law firm, and for the most part, these parents are overjoyed to be reconnected to their children. Kathy, if you'd like, I can run off copies of this, and you can take them with you. It's good to have legitimate proof of your birth records."

"Yes, oh yes, that would be wonderful. Thank you so much for all your help."

"It's my pleasure, Kathy. I love to see families reunited. Now, I'll make some copies, and I'll be right back."

"Janet, are you thinking what I'm thinking? What are the odds of this happening? I can remember hearing that name when I was growing up, maybe at school, I'm not sure. Do you think it's the same Lombardo family that your daughter is connected to?"

"I think it could very well be, unless there is more than one Marco Lombardo, which I doubt. I could call Paula and ask her what Daniel's father's name is, if you like?"

"I need to think about this."

Winifred then entered the office with papers in hand. "Kathy, I hope this report helps you find your family. Now, if there is anything else I can do, don't hesitate to call, and please let me know how you make out. I wish you all the best in your search, and again, if there is anything else I can do, just give me a call."

"Thank you, Winifred, and yes, I'll let you know as soon

as I find them.”

Janet was a little concerned about Kathy. She was so quiet during the drive home in the cab, clutching the envelope to her chest. Janet even saw a tear roll down her cheek.

Entering the apartment, Janet offered to make tea. “Kathy, I can only imagine how difficult this must be for you. Let’s have some tea, and try to focus on the good that’s come from all this.”

“Janet, I don’t even know where to start. What do I do with this? How should I contact them? My God, what if they don’t want anything to do with me?”

“Kathy, I’ve met Daniel, and he came across as a very nice young man, kind and caring. I’m sure he would be delighted to know that he has a half-sister, and his dad would probably be over the moon to be in touch with his daughter.”

“Oh, Janet, do you really think so?”

“Well, there’s only one way to find out. You could check out the law firm that Daniel and his father own.”

“Yes, that’s a great idea. I just don’t know what to say. What do you say… ‘Hi, I’m your sister???’”

“How about if we asked Winifred to arrange a meeting at her office?”

“Yes, that sounds perfect. I’ll call her.”

CHAPTER TWENTY-FIVE

"Morning, Dad. I thought I'd go in early this morning. There's something I'm looking into for a client; apparently, something unexpected came up yesterday. I told him I'd get on it right away."

Not wanting his wife to be aware, Marco responded with a wink and said, "Sure, son, I think I'm familiar with the case. I'll be along shortly."

"See you at the office, Dad."

Daniel's mum entered the kitchen. "Okay, Marco, stop playing games. Daniel knows, you told him, didn't you?"

"I had no choice after the scene you made. Not to mention, he has a right to know that he has a sister out there."

"You mean half-sister, and if she's anything like her mother, he's better off without her!"

"Audrey, you have to realize what happened wasn't her fault, and if Daniel wants to find her, that's his choice. Must you always be so insensitive?"

"I don't mean to be, it's just that I don't like this coming back to life. I'd hoped it was dead and buried!"

"It's Mary who's dead and buried, but her daughter… my daughter, is still alive, and I'm going to find her, regardless of what you think. For God's sake, Audrey, have a heart!"

Daniel sat waiting in the office, wondering what was keeping his dad and hoping his parents weren't having another heated discussion about finding his sister. He decided to take the initiative and call the office of the Foster Care System there in Boston and book an appointment for him and his Dad. He couldn't believe his luck; due to a cancellation, they had an opening that afternoon at three o'clock. Daniel was so excited, he couldn't wait to tell his dad.

Arriving at the Foster Care office, Daniel and his dad were both a little on edge, not knowing what they would find out or how long it would take to know anything. They didn't have to wait long; the social worker was right on time. After inviting them in to take a seat, she kindly asked, "Now, gentlemen, how can I help?"

After a brief explanation of what took place thirty-seven years ago, Marco was feeling doubtful that they would find her after all this time. "I understand these things take time," he said, "and at her age, she could be anywhere. She could be married, or God forbid, she might not even be alive."

"Mr. Lombardo, you must remain hopeful. Yes, it's been a long time since she was in the System, but we will do everything in our power to help, and if that doesn't work, you could always hire a detective."

"Yes, I did think about hiring a detective, but I thought I would start here, and maybe find out where her last foster care home was, and maybe they would know where she went from there?"

"Well, Mr. Lombardo, I promise you, we will do everything in our power to reunite you with your daughter."

It had only been a week when Daniel and his dad received a call from Foster Care, telling them they had information regarding their case. Daniel and his dad were over the moon; they could hardly wait to hear what she had to say.

Again, Daniel and his dad waited outside the Foster Care office, too excited to talk; they were so looking forward to what she was about to tell them, hoping and praying it would be good news.

Daniel and his dad looked up after hearing, "Mr. Lombardo, please come in and take a seat, you as well, Daniel. I have something that was brought to my attention when I began the search for your daughter. It appears that the Foster Care System in New York has contacted our office here in Boston. She... Kathy O'Brien has laid charges against a former foster parent. Also, before we get to that, she has recently been searching for her biological family, who she believes are from the Boston area."

Daniel and his dad turned to each other with shock on their faces. Then, turning to the counselor, they both asked, "So she must be in New York, and she is looking for us?"

"Yes, she recently started searching for family, and she's lived in New York City since leaving foster care."

Daniel asked, "So you say her name is Kathy O'Brien; therefore, she goes by her mother's name, and she must not be married, is this correct?"

"Yes, that is correct. Mary O'Brien, being single at the time of the birth, gave the baby her last name. Also, we do have a contact number where she can be reached: MACY'S DEPARTMENT STORE in New York City. She mentioned that it was her private office number."

With big smiles on their faces, Daniel and his dad were so excited to receive this information so soon. "This is wonderful news!" Marco exclaimed. "So what should we do now? Should we reach out to her, or wait for her to come looking for us?"

"Well, that's entirely up to you. Considering she's searching for family, I think you should try to contact her. I can give you the number where you can reach her. Also, now that DNA testing is available, there is a chance she might want a DNA sample, just to be sure."

Marco looked both joyful and concerned. "Yes, I have no problem with doing a DNA test. Actually, it's probably for the best. Now, what about the abuse that she suffered from the foster parent? Have there been charges laid? I sincerely hope so."

"Actually, it has been brought to the attention of the Foster Care System, and the police have been notified. I'm sorry, but I'm not in a position to divulge any of that information.”

“I understand, and I’m sure that when we find Kathy, she will let us know. Especially if she needs a lawyer.”

“Here is the number where you can reach Kathy. I hope this all works out well for you.”

“Yes, me too. Thank you for all your help in leading us in the right direction in finding my daughter.”

“Glad I could help, please keep me informed of your progress.”

Daniel was so excited after leaving the Foster Care Office. “Dad, this is amazing. When do you think we should reach out to Kathy?”

“Well, I’m thinking we could call anytime, and maybe arrange to meet on the weekend. What do you think?”

“I think that sounds perfect, Dad. Why don’t we go back to the office and see if we can reach her?”

“It’s a little late in the day, son. She may be gone for the day. I think I’ll wait until tomorrow. This is a lot to take in, not to mention how I’m going to tell your mother.”

“Oh, I’m sure you can handle this, and I think mum will come around in time.”

“I sincerely hope so. This is huge, Daniel. My head is spinning. I need to go home and grab a glass of Scotch. Care to join me?”

"Absolutely, I could use a drink myself."

Just as they were about to leave the office, the phone rang. Marco picked up. "Hello, Lombardo Law. Yes, this is he, yes… yes, I'm in the process of searching for my daughter. Really? Oh my, yes, yes of course. No, that wouldn't be a problem at all. I can come to New York, just say when. This coming Monday, I'll be there, and my son will be with me as well. Thank you, thank you so much, I'll see you Monday.

"Dad, was that call what I think it was?"

"It was indeed. You and I are going to New York on Monday."

CHAPTER TWENTY-SIX

Janet was looking forward to going home for Thanksgiving. She just wished things weren't so hectic. Oh, the realization that Daniel could be Kathy's brother was mind-blowing. She wondered if they would do one of those DNA tests that just came out. It would certainly prove they're related. Her thoughts then turned to Ruth. She couldn't help feeling guilty for not keeping in touch more. She thought that, hopefully, when Kathy's situation gets all confirmed, things would quiet down. Then again, there was the matter of telling Paula that Ruth was her grandmother. She then spoke out loud, "Oh, what a tangled web we weave."

Arriving back at the apartment with take-out for supper, Janet was pleased to see Kathy was home. "Kathy, I'm back, hope everything is okay at work?"

"Oh, Janet, hi… yeah, everything is fine with work, my staying late was due to a call I received from the Foster Care System. I just needed some alone time to clear my head after speaking to the counselor."

"Oh, Janet, I hope she gave you good news."

"Actually, it's very good news… I'm going to meet my father and brother on Monday, but there was something else she informed me of."

"Really, what else did she say?"

"It was about the complaint I made to the Foster Care System."

"Yes, what did she tell you?"

"She told me Child Protective Services did a thorough search, and they discovered that the name of the person whom I accused of abuse is now deceased. Can you believe that? Deceased? My God, he got away with it. Oh, why didn't I report it long ago?"

"Kathy, I know you're upset, but you have to see this from a different perspective. It's probably for the best; otherwise, you may have had to lay charges and make a court appearance. This way, you can put it behind you for good, or there is counselling available if you choose. Whatever you think is best for you."

"Oh, Janet, I don't know what I would do without you. You're like the sister I never had."

"Kathy, you just made my day. Now, I'm going to suggest we concentrate on you meeting your wonderful family, who I'm sure can't wait to meet you. You must be so excited. I know I am."

"Yes, Janet, I'm very excited, and I'm hoping you will come with me. I don't think I could do this on my own."

"Kathy, I would never let you do this alone. I'll be right beside you all the way."

CHAPTER TWENTY-SEVEN

Monday morning arrived with a blue sky and a feeling of fall in the air. Daniel and his dad were pleased to see a clear day, considering they had a long drive from Boston to New York. They both agreed it was best not to let on to Audrey why they were driving to New York. They led her to believe it was work-related, just in case she wondered why they were late coming home.

Arriving in New York, they made their way to the office of the Foster Care System. They could barely contain their excitement. Approaching a lady at the front desk, Marco introduced himself and Daniel, explaining they had an appointment to meet with Winifred White.

"Oh, yes, follow me, I'll take you to her office." The lady knocked on the door, then, opening it, she announced their arrival. Entering the office, the lady behind the desk came forward, extending her hand, saying, "I'm Winifred White, and you must be Marco and Daniel Lombardo. I'm so pleased to meet you both."

Marco spoke up, "Yes, it's nice to meet you as well. My son and I are both very excited that this day has arrived, and I have to confess, I'm not sure if I could have waited any longer."

"That's quite understandable, Mr. Lombardo. It's

exciting for us here at Foster Care as well. It's always a pleasure to bring families together. Now, follow me, and I'll take you both to meet your daughter and sister. She's been waiting for you."

As they followed Winifred down the hall, they entered a lovely room, where two ladies were seated. Daniel and his dad were wondering which one was Kathy. Winifred spoke up as soon as she entered, saying, "Kathy, would you please stand and meet your biological father and your brother?"

Kathy was quick to rise from her chair, then reached out with open arms, and her dad did the same. They embraced, with tears in their eyes, and they both reached out to Daniel. The three of them stood there in a warm embrace, saying, "I'm so happy I found you."

Winifred, who was also feeling the emotion in the room, spoke up, "Why don't we take a seat?"

Janet, who remained seated, couldn't stop smiling; it took her back to the day when Paula turned up at her parents' front door.

Just then, Daniel recognized Janet, who was still sitting quietly in the chair. "Wow, Janet, I didn't expect to see you here. Are you a friend of Kathy's?"

"Actually, we're more than friends; we're roommates."

Meanwhile, Marco and Kathy were chatting away. Marco told Kathy, "My God, Kathy, you're the image of your mother. If I had seen you on the street, I would have known you were my daughter."

Kathy, still wiping tears, replied, "Really? That is so nice to hear. I don't suppose you have a picture of my mother?"

Smiling, Marco replied, "Not on me, but I think I can find one."

Daniel then said to his dad, "Dad, this is Janet, Kathy's roommate, and she is also… Paula's mum."

"I've always said, we live in a small world, and this certainly proves it."

Winifred said, "I'm so happy for you all, but I have to be sure that everyone is satisfied with the outcome, so, if there are any doubts, there is DNA testing available."

Marco stood up and said, "I don't need a DNA test to prove Kathy's my daughter; she is the image of Mary O'Brien, her mother."

"Yes, Mr. Lombardo, that may be, but Kathy might want definite proof of the paternal connection. All it requires is a simple blood test, which we can do here, and you would have the results in a couple of days. That would then certify that you are indeed Kathy's biological father."

Daniel couldn't help thinking of his mother, who would no doubt question the relationship without proof. He looked over at his Dad, and he assumed he was thinking the same thing as he nodded. Marco then turned to Kathy, saying, "I'm okay with doing a test, Kathy, if you are?"

Kathy nodded and said, "Yes, it's probably for the best, just in case we should ever need proof of our lineage."

Marco and Daniel both agreed, it was probably for the best.

After Marco and Kathy had blood samples taken, Winifred told them she would contact them as soon as she received the report. Marco turned to Winifred, saying, "Thank you, Ms. White. You have been most helpful in every aspect of this case. I look forward to hearing from you."

Marco then turned to the girls and Daniel and asked, "Would you ladies do me the honor of taking you both for lunch?"

With smiles all around, they both agreed, "Yes, that would be lovely."

"Daniel, what do you say we take the girls to Patsy's Italian Restaurant?"

"Great choice, Dad. We can introduce Kathy to our Italian traditions."

After enjoying a lovely meal and having an opportunity to spend some quality time together, Daniel turned to his dad and said, "Dad, as much as I hate to end this, we do have a long drive back to Boston."

Kathy, still feeling overwhelmed, turned to Marco and said, "I can't begin to tell you how much this day has meant to me. I am beyond happy that we found each other.”

Marco stood up to give Kathy a hug and then asked, “When can I see you again? We have so much catching up to do.”

“I’m not sure, but I will be in New England for the Thanksgiving weekend. Janet’s sister Jane has invited me to come with Janet and her Aunt Ruth. Maybe we could arrange a meeting then?”

“Yes, that sounds like a wonderful idea. I’ll be in touch, and Daniel and his fiancée Paula will also be at the dinner, so you two can see each other as well.”

“Yes, I expect we will. Oh, this is so exciting!”

Daniel insisted on driving the girls to their apartment building. On arriving, there were hugs and some tears, but they were happy tears, with promises of “I’ll see you soon.”

Entering their apartment, Kathy and Janet were over the moon. They stood and hugged, then hugged again. “Oh, Kathy, I am so happy for you! This is amazing! You know what this means? You and I will have a FAMILY connection!”

“Janet, how in heaven’s name is this all happening? I can hardly wrap my head around all this. I’ll never sleep tonight.”

“Me either, Kathy, so glad tomorrow is our day off.”

Monday morning, Kathy received a call from Winifred, telling her she had received the results of the DNA test.

"Kathy, you're a positive match. Marco Lombardo is your biological father, without a doubt."

"Oh, that's wonderful to hear! Thank you, Winifred, for calling, and for all your help; you've been a Godsend."

"I'm so happy for you, Kathy. I wish you all the best."

Kathy was over the moon hearing the results of the DNA test; she couldn't wait to tell Janet.

CHAPTER TWENTY-EIGHT

Jane was so pleased with how well she felt physically. The doctor did say that being an organ donor can also be beneficial to the donor, as well as the recipient. She felt totally recovered and couldn't wait to start planning the Thanksgiving dinner. She was a little unsure of inviting Daniel's parents… Daniel's mother was somewhat pretentious, which made her feel a bit uncomfortable. "I'll wait and see what Bobby thinks," she decided. "Oh, I need to call Janet to find out when they will be arriving."

Picking up the phone and dialing Janet's number, she was surprised when she answered on the first ring.

"Hello, Janet speaking."

"Hi Janet, it's your sister calling. How are you?"

"Oh, Jane, I couldn't be better. How are you? Keeping well, I hope?"

"Yes, I'm well, thanks… no problems from the surgery, none whatsoever."

"That's great to hear, Jane, after all you have done."

"So tell me, what's got you so upbeat?"

"Well, there's going to be a surprising announcement for everyone on the day of the dinner."

"Really, now my curiosity's piqued. I'm looking forward to hearing it. So, the reason I'm calling is, Dad wants to know when you, Kathy, and Aunt Ruth will be arriving?"

"You can tell Dad we should be there Friday evening, and we'll probably leave work early. I know Ruth doesn't like to drive after dark. I'm so looking forward to seeing you, Jane, and everyone else, too, of course. Is there anything I can bring?"

"Just Kathy and Aunt Ruth. Looking forward to seeing you all. Take care, and see you soon."

"You too, Jane, love you, sis."

After hanging up the phone, Jane couldn't help but smile. Janet had become a totally different person, and all for the good. She then felt a warm, peaceful sensation, and she just knew it was her mom.

Bobby arrived home feeling upbeat. "Hi Jane, I'm home, I have news."

"I'm in the living room, Bobby."

After kissing Jane on the cheek, Bobby announced, "I have good news. You don't have to worry about inviting Daniel's parents to the dinner. Daniel called me at work today to tell me how much he and Paula were looking forward to it, and also that his dad was taking his mom away for the weekend. Something about his dad wanting to mend fences with his wife."

"That is good news, Bobby. I didn't want there to be any awkward vibes at the table. I spoke with Janet earlier, and she and Kathy are very excited about coming to the dinner."

"Wonderful. Now Jane, what can I do to help?"

"I could use some help with the shopping."

"I can do that, just say when."

CHAPTER TWENTY-NINE

It was a beautiful November day, perfect for Thanksgiving. Jane couldn't help remembering all the Thanksgiving dinners her mom had prepared over the years. Thinking back, she now understood why Aunt Ruth always had an excuse for not being there. Hopefully, she thought, "We can put all the secrets behind us soon." She couldn't help feeling sorry for Aunt Ruth, who still hasn't been able to tell Paula, she is her grandmother; maybe that was what Janet was referring to as her big announcement. "I guess we'll find out today." Jane finished setting the table, adding a fall centerpiece and the final touch, her mother's favorite candle holders. She was pleased with the outcome. The meal was all ready except for the turkey, which only needed to be carved.

Jane shouted out to Bobby, who was in the den, "Bobby, would you please carve the turkey while I go upstairs to get changed?"

"I'll get right on it, Jane. Everything looks great, and smells good too."

Just as Jane was coming downstairs, she heard the doorbell ring. Opening the door, she was happy to see Bobby's parents standing there. With a big smile, Jane welcomed them to come inside.

"Bobby, your mom and dad are here. Oh, and here comes Paula and Daniel, and Dad with Aunt Ruth, and Janet, and that must be Janet's friend Kathy. Welcome, welcome, please come in, make yourself at home. We're so happy you all could make it."

After all the hugs and greetings, Janet introduced Kathy to Bobby and Jane, Paula and Daniel, and Bobby's Parents. Once all the introductions were made, Jane suggested they all take a seat in the dining room.

Liam then spoke up, "Considering this is Thanksgiving, and that we have so much to be thankful for, I'd like to say grace, if that's okay with everyone."

Everyone agreed and bowed their heads as Liam gave thanks for his family and for being reunited with Paula. As soon as the Amen was said, Jane said, "Let's eat before it gets cold."

After everyone was finished, they all proclaimed how delicious the meal was. Jane replied with a grateful "thank you," suggesting they all go into the living room and have a toast to family. "Bobby, would you get the wine, please? And I'll get the glasses."

As they all raised a glass, Daniel said, "I'd like to make a toast."

Everyone raised their glass; Daniel cleared his throat and, with profound emotion in his voice, said, "I know you have all been introduced to Kathy, but what you're not aware of is that Kathy and I, just recently discovered, that we are brother and sister!" Raising his glass, Daniel looked towards Kathy and said, "To family!"

Everyone was so surprised, but in the best way. With hugs, smiles, and congratulations all around, Janet began tapping her glass. "This is wonderful news, and I couldn't be happier for Kathy and Daniel."

Turning to Paula, Janet became emotional and said, "Paula, I can't begin to tell you how much it has meant to me to have you in my life. Therefore, I feel this is the perfect time to introduce you to your grandmother, whom I grew up believing was my aunt, but is actually my biological mother."

Ruth stepped up, hugging Janet and Paula. Overwhelmed with joy, Paula said, "I never dreamed I would ever see the day when I would have a grandmother. I'm feeling so blessed to have found my forever family. Now, we need to raise our glasses again." Motioning Daniel to stand with her, they both announced together, "We've set a date for the wedding… New Year's Eve."

Liam then spoke up, "I'm delighted for all of you, and the best part is, there are no more secrets. We are all family, and that's all that matters, and family will always come first. Let's raise a glass to family and to Anne, whom I know in my heart is looking down and smiling too, as we all are."

Bobby's dad, Robert, taking this all in, leaned into Bobby and whispered, "Son, we need to go for coffee soon, so you can explain all this."

With a knowing smile on his face, Bobby replied, "Sure, Dad, sure, just say when."

9 781970 563467